HAIRY HETTIE

Illustrated by

JO ALLAN

Picture Kelpies

Hettie the Highland cow lived in Scotland on Granny Macleod's farm. Granny had two grandchildren, Callum and Kirsty, who liked to visit Hettie.

It was spring, and the sun was shining. Hettie was in her field, having a tasty breakfast of grass and dandelions.

It was usually cold in Scotland, so Hettie's coat was thick and hairy to keep her warm.

Two blackbirds flew by looking for a place to make their nest. *Chirrup, chirrup, tweet!* they said, and they started to build a nest in Hettie's hair.

Mooooo said Hettie. She wasn't sure about this. She was a cow not a hedge.

But the blackbirds were happy with their new home, and they settled down to lay their eggs.

It was summer, and Hettie was hot under her thick coat. But she had lots of lovely flowers to eat.

The blackbirds were singing happily, *Chirrup, chirrup, tweet!* Their eggs had hatched and the baby birds were learning to fly.

Some butterflies fluttered around Hettie's head, and landed on her nose, which was very tickly.

Moo

oo - choooooO!

Hettie let out a big sneeze. She hoped
the butterflies would fly away soon.
She was a cow not a leaf.

  But the butterflies had found a new
home. They settled on Hettie's fur and
laid their eggs, which soon hatched
into wriggling caterpillars.

It was autumn, and it was very windy. Hettie was trying to eat brambles from the hedge.

The blackbirds were singing as they mended their nest, *Chirrup, chirrup, tweet!*

The caterpillars had turned into brand new butterflies, but it was much too windy to fly.

A squirrel scurried by looking for a place to hibernate for the winter.

Sniffle, sniffle, squeak! said the squirrel as it
snuggled down in Hettie's long fur.

MOOOOO

said Hettie grumpily. She was a cow not a tree.
But the squirrel was already fast asleep.

It was winter, and it was freezing cold outside. But underneath her hairy coat, Hettie was very warm indeed.

And so were the blackbirds,
who were having a snooze.

And the butterflies, who were
hiding, fast asleep.

And the squirrel, who was
snoring, *Snort, snort, snaaarf!*

Along came a mountain
hare, who was tired of
looking for food in
the snow.

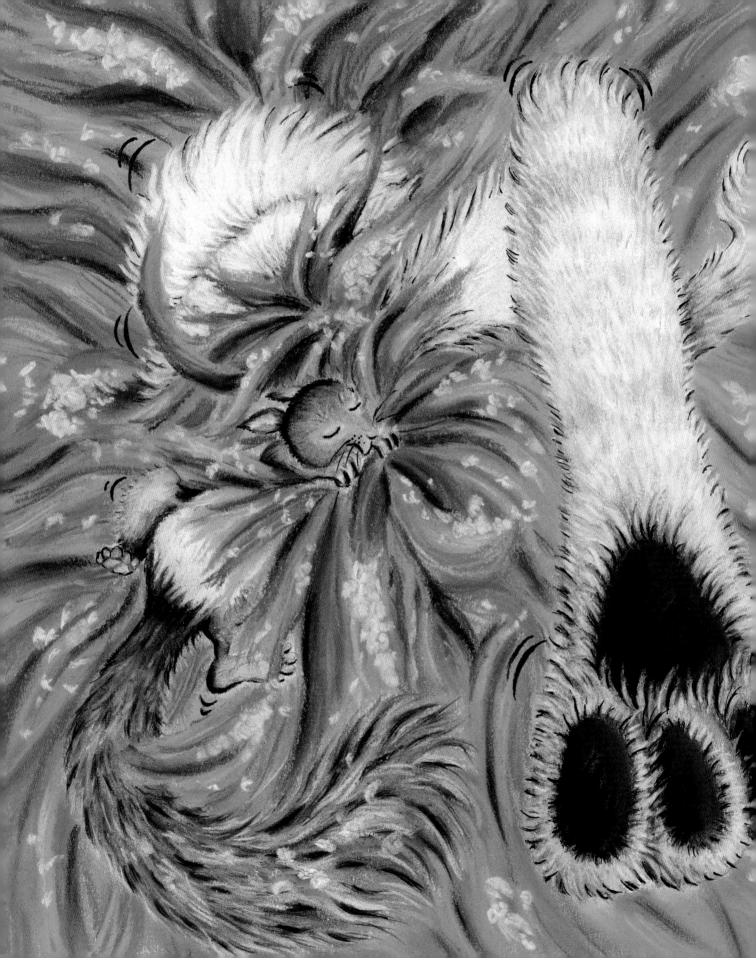

Boiiinng!

The hare hopped onto Hettie's back and burrowed into her thick fur.

Mooooo!

said Hettie, as the hare kicked her with its strong back legs. She was a cow not a walking zoo!

Hettie shook her coat, but all the animals hung on tightly.

It was nearly spring, and Hettie was feeling itchy.
   The blackbirds were flapping.
   The butterflies were fluttering.
   The squirrel was twitching.
   And the hare gave Hettie an almighty kick,

THUMP!

This was the final straw. As fast
as she could, under the weight
of all the animals, Hettie
trotted over to
Granny's cottage.

MOOOOOOOOOOO!

Hettie bellowed.

Granny Macleod and Callum and
Kirsty rushed outside.

"Oh, Hettie! What a mess!" said
Granny. She sometimes had bad
hair days herself, but never
quite like this.

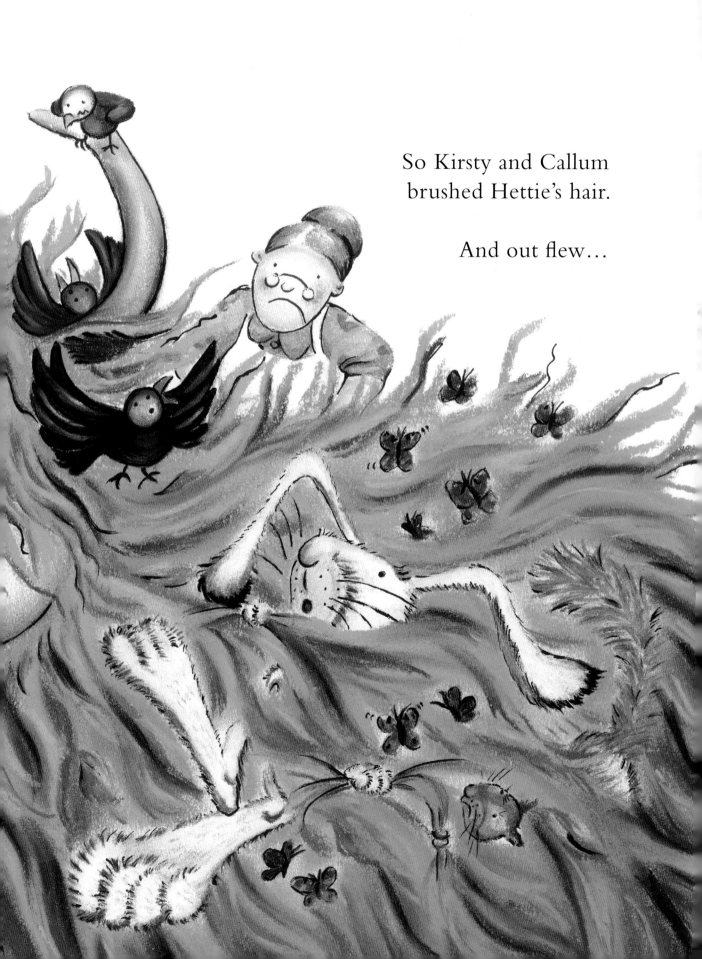

So Kirsty and Callum
brushed Hettie's hair.

And out flew…

...two blackbirds,

lots of pretty butterflies,

a sleepy squirrel,

and a startled mountain hare.

"All these creatures have been sleeping in Hettie's hair!" said Callum.

"She's a cow not a hairy hotel!" said Kirsty.

"Poor Hettie," said Granny. Then she got out the shears and gave Hettie a good trim.

Hettie liked her new haircut. But where had all the animals gone?

The blackbirds were building a nest
in the hedge.
The butterflies were flying among the
leaves.
The squirrel was making its nest in a tree.
And the mountain hare was hopping
back up the hillside.

Mooooo

said Hettie,
happy at last.